This book belongs to

_____

To Sula and Barney,
Georgie and Fudge...
and anyone else who
knows me. - Lola 🐾

To Scot and Neil, my big ~~bothers~~
(I mean BROTHERS!) - lindsey x.

OXFORD
UNIVERSITY PRESS

Great Clarendon Street, Oxford OX2 6DP

Oxford University Press is a department of the University of Oxford.
It furthers the University's objective of excellence in research, scholarship,
and education by publishing worldwide in

Oxford   New York

Auckland Bangkok Buenos Aires Cape Town Chennai Dar es Salaam Delhi Hong Kong
Istanbul Karachi Kolkata Kuala Lumpur Madrid Melbourne Mexico City Mumbai Nairobi São Paulo
Shanghai Taipei Tokyo Toronto

Oxford is a registered trade mark of Oxford University Press in the UK and in certain other countries

Text and illustrations © Lindsey Gardiner 2004

The moral rights of the author / artist
have been asserted

Database right
Oxford University Press (maker)

First published 2004

British Library Cataloguing in Publication Data available

ISBN 0-19-278223-1 (hardback)   ISBN 0-19-272572-6 (paperback)

10 9 8 7 6 5 4 3 2 1

Printed in Singapore
Colour reproductions by Dot Gradations Ltd, UK

THE LOOPY LIFE OF Lola!

LINDSEY GARDINER

OXFORD
UNIVERSITY PRESS

The following events are based on a true story. Any resemblance to real-life characters is NOT a coincidence.
No names have been changed to protect the (not so) innocent!

Meet LOLA!

She's my lively,

sometimes a bit loopy,

but ALWAYS
LOVABLE dog!

D - O - G ...
DOG!

Now I know she's a dog

and YOU know

she's a dog,

but LOLA has OTHER IDEAS!

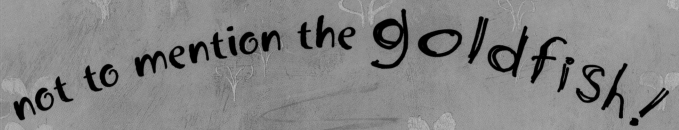

(Lucky he's a fast swimmer!)

OUTSIDE...

At home, she's a little

MOUNTAIN
GOAT

jumping from peak ...

to peak ..

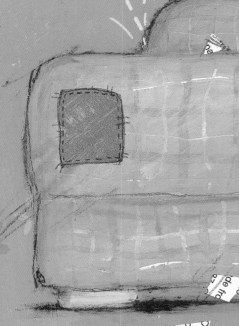

with her AMAZING balancing act

and
EATING
EVERYTHING
she
finds
a
l
o
n
g
the
way!

munch
munch

At mealtimes, LOLA'S a
FUSSY little madam!
(She seems to think she's human.)

She INSISTS
on having
the SAME as
everyone else ...

...no matter
how messy!

(And at the table,
of course.)

SOMETIMES ...

...LOLA is just like a LITTLE PRINCESS,

perched on her puffy pillow ...

...with everyone **FUSSING** over her!

She just LOVES that!

In the park, LOLA is a little lamb, BOUNCING and SPRINGING her way

Boing…

boing…

Bbzzzzz

through the daisies!

Sometimes LOLA'S
a mischievous
little MAGPIE...

...trailing TREASURES

back to her **nest!**

... is when she's just **LOLA**,

my lively,

sometimes a bit loopy

buzzzzz

but ALWAYS LOVABLE little dog!

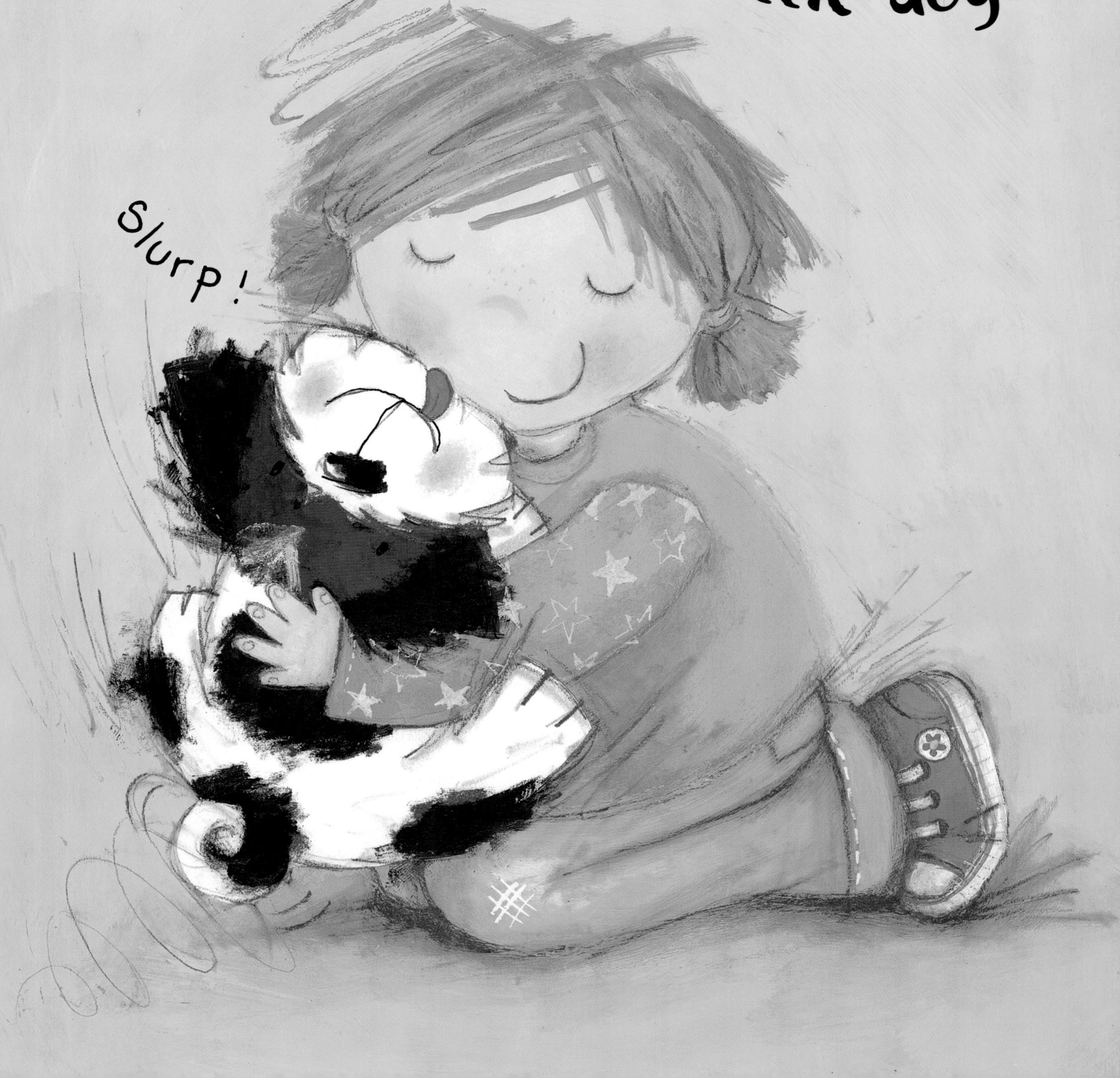

And that's when
I love her MOST.

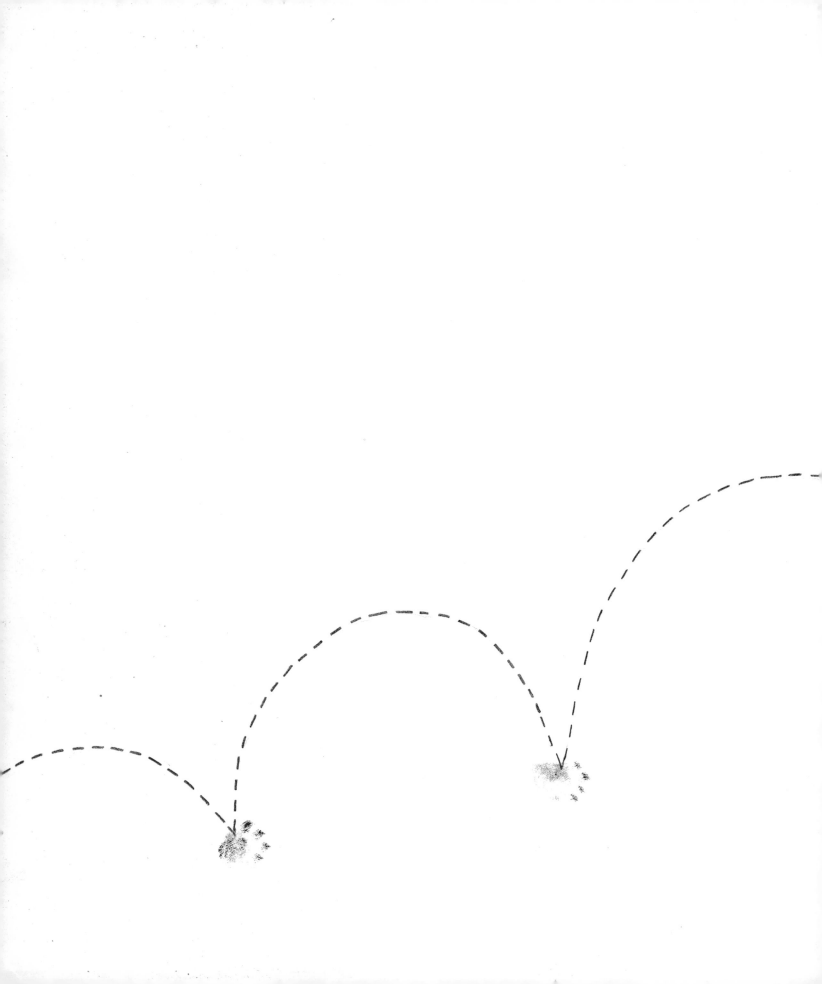